VOLUME ONE

A Child's Gift of Bedtime Stories™

BY

GARRY CHAFFIN & LINDA BURNSED

ILLUSTRATED BY

TERESA B. RAGLAND

THOMASSON-GRANT
CHARLOTTESVILLE

To Richmond—GC.
To Justin, Christopher, Aaron, Bethany, and Brian—LFB.
Special thanks to David R. Lehman and Isabel D. Landeo
for their help and encouragement.

Published by Thomasson-Grant, Inc.

Copyright © 1993 Thomasson-Grant, Inc.
Text and illustrations copyright © 1993 S, C & B, a Tennessee partnership
comprised of Someday Baby, Inc., R. Garry Chaffin and Linda F. Burnsed.
All rights reserved.
A Child's Gift of Bedtime Stories is a trademark of Someday Baby, Inc.

00 99 98 97 96 95 94 93   5 4 3 2 1

Any inquiries should be directed to Thomasson-Grant, Inc.
One Morton Drive, Suite 500, Charlottesville, Virginia 22903-6806
(804) 977-1780

Library of Congress
Cataloging-in-Publication Data
Chaffin, Garry
    A child's gift of bedtime stories / by Garry Chaffin and Linda Burnsed ; illustrated by
Teresa Ragland.
        p.   cm.
    Contents: Tomorrow we'll go to the fair -- Wings -- Hushabye Street -- Lullaby for
Teddy.
    ISBN 1-56566-044-7 : $13.95
    [1. Friendship--Fiction. 2. Bedtime--Fiction.] I. Burnsed, Linda,. II. Ragland, Teresa, ill.
III. Title.
PZ7.C3484Ch 1993
[E]--dc20   93–17766
                                                                                                         CIP
                                                                                                          AC

❧ CONTENTS ❧

TOMORROW WE'LL GO TO THE FAIR

The spray from the lawn sprinkler created a colorful rainbow against the bright blue sky. Shirley and Andy pretended to be at the beach, while Andy's dog, Mischief, bathed in the rays of the warm September sun.

"Let's see who can sit on top of the beach ball the longest," Andy challenged. The two friends took turns straddling the brightly colored ball, holding their arms out like airplane wings to balance themselves. But the wet ball was too slick, and they soon tumbled feet over head onto the soft ground. They lay there giggling, when suddenly two figures towered above them.

"Andy and Shirley, I'd like you to meet Laura." Standing beside Shirley's mom was a young girl about Shirley's age.

"Laura is spending the weekend with her grandparents — the Thompsons, next door. I thought maybe you'd like to invite her to your beach party!"

1

Laura stood shyly alongside Shirley's mom, not looking up at first. When her mom had gone, Shirley suggested: "Hey Laura, why don't you put on your swimsuit and join us?"

"I don't think so," Laura answered. "My father takes me to the *real* beach." With that, Laura sat down under the big oak tree in Shirley's backyard.

"She sure isn't very friendly!" Shirley whispered to Andy.

"Maybe she's just a little shy," Andy replied.

Andy and Shirley wondered how they might persuade Laura to play with them. Suddenly Andy had an idea.

"Laura, watch out!" he yelled. "It's a dinosaur!"

Andy and Shirley could see the big green grasshopper bounding toward them. There in the grass, at eye level to the insect world, the grasshopper really did look huge. Laura didn't budge, but Shirley instantly played along.

"Help . . . Mischief! It's a dinosaur!" she squealed. Mischief came rushing to their rescue, leaping in the air after the high-jumping bug and scooping up a mouthful of wet grass as he fell flat on his nose!

"Your dog sure is clumsy," Laura remarked. "My dog has a *pedigree* . . . he's not a mutt like yours."

"Shy, huh?" Shirley mumbled to Andy.

"My dad says mixed breeds make good pets," Andy responded, defending his faithful companion. "And besides, I think he looks like a retriever!"

"He looks more like a dodo bird to me!" Laura laughed. "Maybe *he* should be the dinosaur!"

Shirley couldn't bear it any longer. "Let's go, Andy," she demanded. "She can't talk about Mischief like that!"

Shirley and Andy and Mischief left Laura alone under the oak tree.

The next morning Shirley was in her backyard when Laura appeared. Shirley's bear, Teddy, was lying comfortably in a wicker chair with Shirley's doctor bag close at hand.

"What are you doing?" Laura asked. She seemed friendlier than she had been the day before, but Shirley wasn't sure.

"I'm putting a fresh bandage on Teddy's arm," Shirley replied. Then she added sarcastically, "But I'm sure you have a better bear at your house."

"I don't live in a house," Laura said. "I live in a tall apartment building in the city!"

Before Shirley could respond, Andy and Mischief came rushing around the corner of the house. "Shirley!" Andy screamed. "It's the fair! Hurry! You've got to see it!"

With her stethoscope still hanging from her neck, Shirley ran after Andy, leaving Laura all alone.

When Shirley and Andy reached the intersection at the end of the street, Shirley couldn't believe her eyes. A policeman had the usual traffic stopped for a caravan of trucks. Neighborhood children began to gather on both sides of the street, while truck after truck passed, hauling the most wonderful cargo! There were model airplanes and boats of all colors — big enough to ride in. On the side of one truck were the words "SNOW CONES" and "COTTON CANDY." Another looked like a fun house on wheels. The men in the big trucks waved to the children, who cheered with delight.

At last Shirley spotted what she had been waiting for — the carousel! Staring at the painted ponies, she imagined sitting in their colorful saddles — gliding up and down to the happiest music in the world.

As the carousel rolled out of sight, Shirley and Andy turned to see Laura standing far behind them. "Oh no," Shirley said, "I forgot about Laura!"

"Laura," Shirley yelled, "wait up! Did you get to see the fair?"

"That's nothing." Laura said as Andy and Shirley joined her. "The *circus* comes to our city — it's got elephants and clowns and everything!"

"Yeah," Andy replied, "but I bet it doesn't have rides and cotton candy! The fair starts tomorrow. Would you like to go with us?"

"I'm going home tomorrow!" Laura answered. Then she turned and ran toward her grandparents' house.

"Good riddance," Andy said.

Shirley paused, then whispered, "I think she was crying."

That evening, Shirley and Andy were watching fireflies flicker, when Shirley's grandpa pulled up in his red pickup truck. In the back of the pickup were two very large watermelons.

"Want to go with me to the fairgrounds?" her grandpa shouted. "I'm going to enter these melons. I thought you kids might want to watch the men set up the rides."

Andy and Shirley jumped up and down when their parents said they could go. As her grandpa started to pull out of the driveway, Shirley asked, "Grandpa, would it be okay if Laura went with us? She has to go home tomorrow, and I don't think she's ever been to a fair."

"Sure it would!" Grandpa said, and he waited in the truck while Shirley and Andy ran next door to get Laura.

From the moment they arrived at the fairgrounds, Laura trembled with excitement. There were more rides and lights than she had ever seen! It made Shirley happy to see Laura smile.

They were on their way back to grandpa's truck when Laura stopped in front of the carousel. She turned to Andy and Shirley and said, "I wish I could stay and ride with you tomorrow. And . . . I'm sorry if I hurt Mischief's feelings."

"I'll be right back, grandpa," Shirley said. Then she darted toward a man on the other side of the carousel who was turning a bolt with a large wrench. When she returned, the man was right behind her.

"We're almost finished," he said. "All the bolts are tightened and the ponies are ready. There's just one more thing. I need someone to test the ride. Any volunteers?"

Three little hands shot up like lightning! The carousel man winked at Shirley as he helped his volunteers into the gleaming saddles. Then he pulled a lever. Instantly, the lights on the merry-go-round began to flicker, and the multi-colored ponies began to glide. Up and down and around they went to the happiest music in the world.

Later that night as her mom helped her into bed, Shirley said, "Mom, Andy and I have been thinking. You know how sometimes you meet someone and you think you're not going to like them at first? Well, if you give them a second chance, they may become your friend after all."

"Do you know what I think?" Shirley's mom said as she leaned over to kiss her goodnight. "I think you and Andy are growing up."

THE END

WINGS

"What's in the tree?" Andy yelled out as he ran across the lawn. His best friend Shirley was peering up into the elm tree in her backyard. "Cocoons," she replied.

Andy stopped in his tracks. "You mean those furry animals with black rings around their eyes? The ones that wash their food before they eat it?"

"No, silly!" Shirley answered. "You're thinking about raccoons. Cocoons are those little wads of stuff that look like dirty cotton. See?"

Andy tilted his head back. "Wow! Look at all those worms!" he exclaimed.

"Those aren't worms," said Shirley. "Those are caterpillars — there must be hundreds of them."

"What do the cocoons do?" Andy questioned.

"Well," Shirley answered, "Mom says those furry worms — I mean caterpillars — wrap themselves inside the cocoons. And when they come out, they are butterflies, wings and all! Like magic!"

Andy frowned. "You mean those worms grow wings?"
"Yes. But mom said it takes the caterpillars a long time and
a lot of patience," Shirley answered.

Shirley's words were interrupted by the opening of the
back door. "It's dinner time, Shirley," her mom called.
Shirley didn't have to be told twice. "See you later, Andy,"
she yelled as she ran for the back door.

"I guess you're looking forward to your first dance lesson
tomorrow!" Shirley's dad said as they sat down to eat.

"I guess so," she said quietly.

"You don't sound very excited," her mom said. "I thought you wanted to take dance lessons."

"I do . . . it's just that I don't know *how* to dance," Shirley said, teary-eyed.

"None of the children will know how to dance at first," her mom consoled her. "You'll all learn together!"

Shirley's face brightened somewhat. She hoped her mom was right.

The next day Shirley's dance teacher, Miss Betsy, showed the class their first steps. All of the children were clumsy at first, and that made Shirley feel more comfortable. Still, she doubted she would ever be able to dance as well as Miss Betsy.

As soon as Shirley arrived home, she ran over to Andy's house. "Want to see me dance?" she asked him.

"Okay," Andy shrugged.

Shirley carefully moved about, taking one step at a time, just as Miss Betsy had shown her. But she could tell by the look on Andy's face that he was not impressed. "It's hard to do without the music," she explained.

Week by week, Shirley grew more fond of her dance teacher. She knew Miss Betsy liked her, too, because of all the special attention she received. But one thing bothered Shirley: she was never in the right place when the music stopped.

One day on the way home from dance class, Shirley's mom could tell that something was troubling her. "Shirley, is something wrong?" her mom asked.

"I don't think I'm a very good dancer," Shirley answered. "Even the boys are better than me!"

"You're doing fine," her mom assured her. If you concentrate on having a good time, you'll soon be dancing like the little ballerina on your music box!"

Shirley stared out the window the rest of the way home.

Andy was waiting for her on the back porch steps when she arrived. "Don't sit there!" he yelled.

Shirley almost fell as she tried to avoid the caterpillar inching its way across the step. Suddenly, she began to cry.

"It's okay," Andy said. "You didn't sit on him!"

"It's not that," Shirley cried. "All of the other kids can dance . . . except for me. I won't *ever* learn!" Andy thought for a moment, then he touched Shirley's shoulder and smiled. "You know what?" he said, pointing to the caterpillar on the steps. "If those poky little worms can learn to fly, you can learn to dance."

Shirley looked down at the caterpillar patiently making his way and stopped crying.

At dance class the following week, Miss Betsy announced that the students would put on a program for their parents and friends. "Yea!" the children shouted, and they all began

asking questions at once.

"Everyone will have their own part in the program," Miss Betsy said, "but you must keep your part a secret!"

Shirley was so excited that night that she couldn't sleep. Only she and her dance class knew the special part she had been chosen to play. She couldn't tell anyone — not even Andy!

The big day came quickly.

Backstage, Miss Betsy had her hands full keeping all the

little dancers in order. "Remember, boys and girls, stay close to your partner, so you'll be where you're supposed to be when the music stops. And Shirley . . . you just float across the floor wherever you wish. Remember . . . you're the Butterfly! And butterflies flutter from place to place, wherever their beautiful wings can carry them."

Shirley nodded happily. She was the only one in the group who didn't have to keep up with a partner. She could dance wherever she wanted . . . she was the Butterfly!

When the music came to an end, the audience stood and clapped until Miss Betsy closed the curtain for the last time. "You were wonderful, class!" Miss Betsy beamed. "Every one of you!" she said, and she looked right at Shirley.

Moments later, Shirley spotted Andy running toward her. "You had the best part of all!" he exclaimed. "You were the only one who got to dance all over the stage!"

Shirley fell asleep in the car on the way home and didn't awaken until her mom leaned over her to kiss her good night. Sleepily, she asked, "Was I really a good dancer?"

Before her mom could answer, Shirley was asleep again. Her mom held her close and said quietly, "You were the most beautiful butterfly I have ever seen!"

THE END

HUSHABYE STREET

Andy knew that it was time for bed.

The sound of his dog, Mischief, barking at the distant thunder gave Andy an idea. "Mom," he said, "You know how Mischief is afraid of thunder? Well, I've been thinking. Maybe I should stay up for a while, just in case there's a big storm and Mischief needs me."

Andy's mom smiled. "That's very thoughtful of you," she said, "but dad will let him in if he becomes frightened. And besides, it's already past your bedtime. You should be a Sleepy Sam by now — on your way to Dreamland!"

Andy's mom tucked him safely in his warm, comfortable bed. Finding it hard to stay awake, he heard his mom's voice drifting softly away. "Good night, Sleepy Sam."

Andy had just closed his eyes, when suddenly there appeared beside his bed an oddly dressed man scarcely taller than himself. He had a friendly face and seemed to have just awakened from a long sleep.

"Who are you?" Andy asked.

The drowsy little guy answered:

> A ridiculous question,
> It's quite plain to see.
> Why, I'm Sleepy Sam —
> And who might *you* be?

"I'm Andy and this is my room."
But Sleepy Sam had dozed off again, with his chin resting on the palm of his hand. Abruptly, he awakened. Rubbing his eyes, Sleepy Sam bumped his nose with the giant wristwatch strapped to his skinny arm.

> We've got to get going,
> He said with a yawn.
> I'm under strict orders:
> "Have him back home by dawn!"

"Where are we going?" Andy demanded. Sleepy Sam looked at him impatiently.

> To Dreamland, of course —
> That's where we should be.
> So here, put these on;
> They'll help you to see.

Sleepy Sam handed Andy a pair of brightly colored glasses like his own. In an instant, he and Andy were standing in the center of a beautiful old city. People were bustling by on cobblestone streets, many of them nodding at Andy as if they knew him. Street lamps lit up the city, and lively music filled the air.

"Are we in Dreamland?" Andy shouted.

Sleepy Sam frowned at him and replied:

> With all of the lights
> And commotion so near,
> Just how could you get
> Any sleep around here?

Sleepy Sam stretched. He pulled a crumpled piece of paper from his back pocket, turning it one way and another and then back again. On the paper were hundreds of lines running this way and that, marking the roads in and out of this magical city.

"What are you reading?" Andy asked. Sleepy Sam's face turned red with embarrassment.

Oh this? Don't you worry.
It's just an old map.
I could get there and back
In an afternoon nap.

"What you mean is, we're lost," Andy said with a sigh. "Why were *you* sent to take me to Dreamland if you don't know the way?"

Sleepy Sam explained that the night had been especially busy with a heavy workload of children who couldn't sleep.

The overnight guides
Have all been called out.
The main roads are cluttered
With traffic, no doubt!

To make it to Dreamland
And get any sleep,
We *must* find the place
That's called Hushabye Street!

Unfortunately, Sleepy Sam seemed to be having trouble reading the map.

Andy looked as though he might cry. Sleepy Sam quickly assured him:

Don't panic! I need
Just a moment to ponder.
Why don't you go play
On that swing over yonder?

Sleepy Sam pointed to an enormous playground. Between the huge slide and the giant sandbox was a beautiful silver swing. Andy walked over to take a closer look. "Step right up, young man . . . take a ride to the stars," said a friendly man with very little hair and a very big nose. Andy eagerly sat down in the silver swing and fastened his seat belt. Before he could blink an eye, he was swinging through space, past the moon and the stars. Suddenly he was wide awake. After a few moments, Andy heard his name in the distance.

"Get me down," Andy yelled to the swingkeeper. "My friend is calling me."

Instantly, Andy was back on the ground running to where Sleepy Sam was now fumbling with a book entitled, *How to Get to Dreamland.*

As Andy approached, Sleepy Sam tried to hide the instruction book, which had been no help at all. He stuffed the book into his back pocket and cautioned Andy:

> I should have warned you:
> The rides that you take —
> They all are designed
> To keep you awake.

"Thanks a lot!" said Andy. He wondered if he would ever sleep again.

While Sleepy Sam wandered aimlessly in search of Hushabye Street, Andy spotted a field of ponies playing happily together. But he noticed that all alone to one side, a beautiful black pony was grazing lazily in a patch of gold. The pony was wearing a snow-white saddle and motioned for Andy to come closer.

"Jump on my back, and I'll take you to Dreamland," said the little black pony. "I'll come back for Sleepy Sam." Just before Andy put his foot in the stirrup, Sleepy Sam yelled out:

Oh, by the way,
The black horse eating hay
Is a nightmare, of course.
Stay out of her way!

Andy wanted nothing to do with a nightmare. He rushed back to join Sleepy Sam. Andy was very tired now and wanted only to go to sleep.

"Are we *ever* going to make it to Dreamland?" he asked.

Sleepy Sam was sad that he had disappointed Andy. He splashed cold water on his face from the funny-shaped fountain in the center of this unusual city and said with a determined look:

Don't you worry about
This ridiculous mess.

Why, I've been in *much* bigger
Pickles than this!

As Sleepy Sam was speaking, a herd of sheep passed by.
There must have been thousands. Overhearing their conversation, the leader of the herd spoke up confidently, "Hey
kid! Why don't you try counting us? That's sure to put you
to sleep!"

Andy looked at Sleepy Sam, who was ignoring the sheep
altogether. Sleepy Sam spoke without turning around:

That's such an old trick;
You won't fall asleep.
The sun will come up
While you're counting those sheep.

Andy could see that Sleepy Sam was frustrated. "May I
see the map?" he asked.

Sleepy Sam pulled the crumpled paper from his pocket
and handed it to Andy. To Andy's surprise, there it was!
Right in the center of the map, in letters as big as could be —
HUSHABYE STREET. "Sleepy Sam!" Andy yelled, "here it is —
HUSHABYE STREET — we're almost there!"

Sleepy Sam glanced drowsily to where Andy was pointing.
He took off his glasses and scratched his head, saying:

Well, what do you know?
Well I do declare!
The trouble is with
These old glasses I wear.
My eye doctor's right:
They need to be changed.
With this old prescription,
I can't see a thing!

Andy and Sleepy Sam burst into screams of laughter. At once they realized Sleepy Sam had been looking at the map *upside down!*

In a flash they were on Hushabye Street, and they walked through the entrance to Dreamland. Andy turned to shake Sleepy Sam's hand, but he was fast asleep on a park bench. Andy covered him with a newspaper he found on the corner of the bench and lay down beside him.

At Andy's house, it had begun to rain, and the thunder had grown louder. Mischief ran for safety under Andy's bed as his dad peeked in to say goodnight. But Andy didn't hear a thing. Andy was in Dreamland.

THE END

LULLABY FOR TEDDY

It was a special day at Shirley's house. Aunt Jenny and Cousin Lisa were coming for a visit, and Shirley and her mom had gone to the airport to meet them. The house was quiet except for the ticking of the Captain Fearless clock in Shirley's room.

Teddy . . . Teddy Bear, that is, watched the hands of the clock as he anxiously awaited the arrival of Shirley and her cousin.

Teddy was nervous about meeting Lisa for the first time. From his position on Shirley's pillow, he examined his tattered image in the mirror over Shirley's dresser.

"I'm not getting any younger," he thought to himself. "Just look at this tear in my arm. The stuffing around my middle is all lumpy, and the fur on my head is nearly all worn off — I'll be bald before I know it! What if Shirley decides to trade me in for a new bear?"

Teddy's own thoughts took him by surprise. The possibility of being traded in for a new bear had never occurred to him before!

Teddy quickly looked around the room at Shirley's collection of stuffed animals and toys. Then he calmly considered his place of honor on Shirley's bed, next to her favorite blanket.

"I'm being silly," he reassured himself. "No one could take my place." Teddy breathed a sigh of relief remembering when, not so long ago, Shirley had cried and cried, certain her Teddy was lost forever. Actually, he was missing for only a short time before Shirley's mom safely retrieved him from the laundry room.

Teddy's thoughts were interrupted by the sound of footsteps running down the hall toward him.

". . . and this is my room!" he heard Shirley say as the door swung open. In walked Shirley and Lisa. Shirley jabbered excitedly as she showed her cousin around her room, but Teddy hardly heard a word she said. His one button eye was fixed on the big, brown, furry new bear Lisa was holding in her arms!

Then Teddy heard his name. ". . . and *this*," Shirley said, "is my old bear, Teddy. Here, let's put Sebastian next to him on the pillow while I take you to meet Andy, my best friend I was telling you about. He lives across the street."

"On the pillow!" thought Teddy. "This is an outrage! This is *my* special place on Shirley's bed!"

Teddy grimaced as Shirley placed the big furry new bear next to him, blocking his view of the window and Shirley's backyard where he often watched her and Andy play.

The girls left, and once again the only sound in the room was the constant ticking of the clock.

Finally, Sebastian spoke up. "I say, old fellow, this is a grand view you have here." "Who are you calling old?" Teddy snapped. "And the name is Teddy!"

"Teddy?" Sebastian responded thoughtfully. "What a simple name for a teddy bear. Why, it's like having no name at all. It's like calling a cat "kitty" or a dog "puppy.""

"What would you know about names?" Teddy retorted. "You've still got a price tag behind your ear — and I'd say someone paid too much!"

Fortunately, the argument between the bears was interrupted when Shirley and Lisa came running into the room.

"I know my doctor bag is around here somewhere," cried Shirley. "Teddy and I were playing with it just yesterday."

If Teddy could have, he surely would have given Sebastian a knowing wink. Playing doctor was his and Shirley's favorite game. He couldn't wait to see the look on Sebastian's face when Shirley picked him up and carried him outside to play.

Sebastian would have to watch from the window while the girls bandaged Teddy's torn arm. "Maybe being the old bear isn't so bad after all!" he thought.

But instead, upon finding her doctor bag under the edge of the bed, Shirley lifted Sebastian from the pillow and ran with him through the doorway and outside into the backyard. For once Teddy wished he did not have a window view. He couldn't bear the thought of watching Shirley bandage Sebastian's arm . . . it wasn't even torn!

Teddy could hear lots of talking and laughing coming from outside, but he simply couldn't bring himself to look out the window. He tried to tune out the sounds floating up from the backyard and focused once again on the hands of the clock, straining to hear the sound of the ticking above the laughter of the children outside. It would have been a welcome sound to Teddy now.

"How can I compete with Sebastian?" Teddy thought. "I'm just an old, worn-out bear with an ordinary name. And I didn't even cost much when I was new!"

Just when Teddy thought he couldn't hold back his tears any longer, Shirley ran in and scooped him up into her arms. "Come on, Teddy," she said as they raced out the bedroom door. "We're all ready for you!" In a moment, Shirley bounded out the back door and into the backyard with Teddy in her arms.

"SURPRISE !!!" yelled Andy and Lisa and Shirley with great big smiles on their faces. "HAPPY BIRTHDAY, TEDDY! HAPPY BIRTHDAY!"

Teddy couldn't believe it. Stretched across the swing set was a big banner that read, "Happy Birthday, Teddy." And there stood Andy with his bear, Scruffy, with whom Teddy had played many times before, and Lisa with Sebastian, who seemed to be smiling at Teddy for the first time. And all of them were cheering for Teddy. Even Andy's dog, Mischief, who often teased Teddy by nudging him with his cold, wet nose, was barking what must have been "Happy Birthday" in dog language! In all of the excitement of Lisa's visit, Teddy had completely forgotten that it was his birthday! But Shirley had remembered.

As they sat down to enjoy the birthday cake Shirley's mom had made for them, Teddy glanced over at Sebastian, who had cheerfully joined in the birthday celebration as if they were old friends. "Perhaps I misjudged him," he decided.

That night, Shirley's bed was a little more crowded than usual when Shirley's mom and Aunt Jenny came in to say good night. Sandwiched between Shirley and Lisa were Sebastian and Teddy.

"Don't you think Sebastian and Teddy would be more comfortable tonight with your other stuffed animals?" asked Shirley's mom.

"Oh no," cried Shirley. "I'm sure they wouldn't be able to sleep at all . . . they're used to sleeping in a big bed with us."

Shirley's mom grinned at Aunt Jenny. "How about a lullaby before you girls drift off to sleep?" she asked. "Okay," said Shirley sleepily, "but make it a lullaby for Teddy . . . it's his birthday, you know."

Shirley squeezed Teddy tightly and whispered into his worn-out ear, "I love you, Teddy. No one could ever take your place." By the time Teddy glanced up at Shirley, she was fast asleep. It was then that Teddy could close his one button eye, knowing for certain that he meant as much to Shirley as she did to him.

THE END